By Rose Humphrey Burkett

Teacup Memories

Teacup Memories

By Rose Humphrey Burkett

Teacup Memories | Meredith Etc

By Rose Humphrey Burkett

Published by Meredith *Etc*

Meredith McGee DBA Meredith *Etc*

Meredith *Etc*
1052 Maria Court
Jackson, Mississippi 39204-5151

TEACUP MEMORIES

ISBN: 978-1-7378843-3-0

Cover design by Meredith Coleman McGee
Fiction: poems & short, short stories
6x9" trade back softcover
black & white interior
1st printing
10,403 words - 71 pages

Visit and comment online:
Meredith Etc | Official Site… Shop now for books…

Teacup Memories | Meredith Etc

DEDICATION

I dedicate this book to my parents, the Humphreys and my family: the Paynes, Winters, Browns, Myles, Bradleys, and Winders. I extend a special dedication to Martha Young, Kayrecia Mcneil and Edith Guston for being some of the finest Bible schoolteachers that ever lived. Thank you for being a part of my life.

ACKNOWLEDGEMENTS

I wrote this book as a legacy to my husband, A. Jerry Burkett; my parents, Willie and Julie Humphreys; my children, Trica, Jerosha, and Jacobie Burkett; and my grandchildren: Juan, Jordan, Jalen, Jeremi, Jasmyne, Lauren, and Kyrie. I also acknowledge my siblings: Willie Jr., John, Christine, Earnestine, Dianna, Robert, James, and David.

I thank all my friends, Sumner Hill classmates and my Capitol Street Church family. With all the bumps and bruises, life has been wonderful, and I am blessed to have shared it with you. I acknowledge my late Pastor Isaac Young and my late English teacher Anna Patton, whose instructions helped me stay focused and to live the best life possible.

I pray my book will keep my ideas alive in the hearts of readers. May God bless you all!

Teacup Memories

Advance Praise for *Teacup Memories*

Teacup Memories is the perfect title for this collection of inspirational poems and short stories by author Rose Humphrey Burkett. However, you'll want to fill your coffee mug to the brim before cracking open this ingeniously witty book filled with birds chirping, snowflakes falling, bees dancing, and diamonds glistening!

Alice Thomas-Tisdale, Publisher Emerita, Jackson Advocate

I read Teacup Memories. I definitely enjoyed it. The children's stories will inspire readers to make the impossible possible.

Sammy Winder, NFL Running Back, Denver Broncos, 1982-1990

Rose Humphrey Burkett has written that rare book of poetry and prose that speaks to calm the mind.

Teacup Memories is insightful and mind-boggling. It is essential reading to begin your day and to get motivated as you find strength within.

Janice K. Neal-Vincent (Ph.D.), Journalist, Keynote speaker, Performance artist, Poet

CONTENTS

By Rose Humphrey Burkett

1

POEMS TO ENJOY

Remembering Frankie in the Rain

The rain beats down my windowpane.
It reminds me of the place from where I came.

Rain is sweet, it washes my soul.
It takes away the chill, it takes away the cold.

Listening to the rain and playing with my cousin,
clipping paper dolls that we saved by the dozen,

Thinking what we'll be when we both grow up,
sipping cherry Kool-Aid from my little teacup,

I don't see Frankie 'cause she moved far away.
But I see her in my heart every time there is a rainy day.

Snow on My Pillow

The wind is still as the snow comes down.
It falls so slow; it makes no sound.
It sparkles like a diamond ring.
It makes me wonder where I came from.

It feels so strange as I lie here cold,
It sprinkles on my pillow through a small little hole.
I should get up and brush it away,
and find another place to lay.
But time has stopped, and I feel at ease.
The room is quiet, and all noise has ceased.

Life feels good as I think far ahead.
Will I feel good about the things I said?
or will I just lie here as the night grows old,
and watch the snow through a small little hole.

Note: Written by Rose Burkett, Dec. 10, 1989

Ladies Are What Ladies Do

Ladies are such special beings.
They smell like flowers; they smell like rain.

They bring such joy when there is none.
They make you laugh and want to have fun.

They make you smile when times are hard.
You feel at peace and close to God.

Being ladies are what we do best.
We are put through trials and pass the test.

To be a lady is what's happening now.
Let's stand up ladies and take a BOW!

Self

You strive so hard to do your very best.
But 'self' just seems to fail the test.

You try so hard to be so kind.
But 'self' has something else in mind.

You want to laugh and have some fun.
But 'self' says, "no," you need no one.

You want to visit and help the sick.
But 'self' just has another trick.

You want to reach out to the depressed.
But 'self' says no, go buy a dress.

You want to love and help the poor.
But 'self' says no, no more.

You want to say Lord help me.
But 'self' says no, this must not be.

You turn unhappy and wear a frown.
'cause 'self' has won in tearing you down.

This Place Called Home

Small little window that hangs so low.
Pink beautiful roses by the mailbox, they grow.
Tiny little kitchen that stands alone.
The smell of fresh cookies from this place we call home.

Hours spent cleaning on Saturday morn.
The birds keep singing to the bright morning sun.
The pup barks happily as he chews on a bone.
This is it, this place called home.

Rosha is swinging from her new swing set,
Tasha is screaming "is it breakfast yet?"
Mom is calling on the telephone,
what a place, this place call home.

Neighbors want to borrow every day it seems.
Jerry just chuckles as his gold tooth gleams.
So, this is it as we live right along.
In this place, this place called home.

Note: Written by Rose Burkett in 1986

Thunderstorms

The tap-tap sound of sweet-smelling rain.
The glistering streams down my small windowpane.

The splashing sounds as it reaches the ground,
the thunder clouds and lightening sounds,

the wind-swept trees as the trees flow right along,
the big puffy clouds and the rain covered thorns,

the zigzag of lightening as the storm passes through,
the poor sleepy flowers in the thick white dew,

Thunderstorms are not so bad to me.
They are here for a reason, for a reason you see.

Thank God for the thunderstorms and the rain.
because when it is all over, the sun will come out again.

For You Mother

A beautiful petal from a flower bloom,
the beautiful glow from the setting moon,

The lovely sounds from birds in the air,
the wonderful smell of a fresh cut pear,
for you mother.

The sweet hug - your first grandchild,
the laughter behind the smile,

A morning stroll, a morning swing
lots to do, lots of things,

You make all these a joy to be,
for you mother, mother and me.

My Dad, My Dad

He carried us through when times were bad.
He has been there for us.
My dad, my dad.

He has always been strong,
even when I was a lad.
He pushed us forward.
My dad, my dad.

He likes to have fun,
and maybe a few laughs.
He tries to do good.
My dad, my dad.

Though seldom upset,
he tries to be glad.
He helps who he can.
My dad, my dad.

This man I write about is all that I had.
I love him so dearly,
my dad, my dad.

Note: Written by Rose Burkett June 7, 1988

Life in the Country

The roaring whistle of the wind filled trees,
the continuous humming of the fat bumble bees,

the splashing sounds of the ducks in the pond,
the loud breakfast call of dear old mom,

the beautiful lilies that grow by the bay,
the bumpy roads to school by the way,

the dust from a corn field nearby,
the cry of a bird through the air as it soars,

the screams and cries of the neighbor's little one,
the smell of fresh coffee and the warm morning sun,

the long dusty roads that lead to town,
harvesting the fields until the sun goes down.

the long, long walk down that narrow path,
the happiness we share and all the laughs,

Life in the country is so beautiful and delightful.
I wish you could experience such a beautiful sight.

Things I Love to Love

Cool breeze blowing over my face,
pretty dresses covered with lace,

lovely flowers that smell so fresh,
but roses are the ones I like best.

Soft hands and pretty nails,
lots of balloons and boats that sail,

Bumble Bees with their little stripes,
just buzzing around in perfect sight.

Mystery movies that tickle my brain,
makes me wonder if everyone is insane.

Time spent with the one I love,
looking at the sky and the stars above.

The whistling wind on a cold, cold night,
snow on my roof, what a beautiful sight!

Children laughing and playing all day,
can't understand a word they say.

These things I love, and I love them so,
I take them in my heart everywhere I go.

Remembering What I Forgot

The clean warm sun,
as it shines on my face,
the bright yellow butter cups,
dancing from my vase.

The fresh clean wind,
that blows so cool,
the tears of a child,
on the first day of school.

Planning for the future,
in my high school days,
marching across the stage,
on the 21st of May.

Wedding bells with the man,
I truly love,
beautiful white clouds,
that hang from Heaven above.

Finding Christ as my,
life takes a turn,
taking on the world,
my heart just seems to burn.

All these things I,
have put to rest.
They are all good memories,
some are the very best.

Teacup Memories

I hope I remember,
and remember a lot,
and never forget,
The things I forgot.

2

KIDDY POEMS AND SHORT STORIES

Mommy, Mommy

Mommy, Mommy I have a surprise for you.
I have done everything I thought I could do.

I poured my cereal all over the floor.
I threw my juice upside the door.

I poured my milk all over my head.
It went up my nose and I think I'm dead.

I took off my shoes and underpants too,
and now you have something else to do.

I have broken my rattles and all my toys,
I have been making some awful noise.

So, mommy when you come in my room tonight,
do me a favor, don't turn on the light!

Flowers

The flower from your tiny hands means so much to me.
You pulled some of the petals off,
so, the middle is all I can see.

The flowers are not important,
though the smell just carries me away.
It is the tiny little hands that hold them,
and the tiny words he says.

These are precious moments between mother and son.
I want to write them down to read in the morning sun.

The Sad Little Boy

Big brown eyes and shy little smile,
He stands alone, alone a while.

He looks around but no one is there.
He twiddles his thumbs; he pulls his hair.

He makes a sigh; he hums a tune.
No one is there to fill the room.

He claps his hands and stomps his feet.
He starts to whistle and takes his seat.

He starts to cry, and he cries some more,
because all have gone and locked the door.

Note: Written by Rose Burkett June 9, 1991

Where did the Children Go?

With diamond rings and golden chains,
and bright eyes that glow,
oh where, oh where did the children go?

With heels so high and always good-bye,
and teeth so clean they glow,
oh where, oh where did the children go?

With pants so tight and cars so bright,
and blouses cut too low,
oh where, oh where did the children go?

With clean smooth skin and bulging rear ends,
and Sam, Dave, and Joe,
oh where, oh where did the children go?

They have gone away,
forever and ever,
and never will they be,
those beautiful kids,
whom we loved so dearly,
they were locked away,
and someone threw away the key.

Kids Need Love

From broken dishes to toys on the floor,
from scratched up knees to handprints on the door,

From falling grades to Mother's Day cards,
from chicken pox to monkey bars,

kids need love.

from bicycle wrecks to little white lies,
from kisses and hugs and small good-byes,

from Barbie Dolls to toy row boats,
from playground fights to banana floats,

kids need love.

From growing up to being out on their own,
and starting a new life after leaving home.

From arguments fought from dusk to dawn
to thank you so much, I love you mom.

Kids will always need love.

Growing Up

Tiny little bundles with bright
shiny eyes,
first year's birthday,
was a great,
big surprise.

First day of school is the scariest,
of all,
starting Jr. High on the first,
day of Fall.

Twelve years spent for this,
day of graduation,
all the friends are there,
and all close relations.

College seems good as you,
grow right along,
kissing mom and dad when,
it's time to leave home.

Finding the one you love and,
settling down for marriage,
buying your first home and,
your first baby carriage.

The kids are all grown up,
and the cycle starts again,
tiny little bundle and your,
first diaper pin.

The Little Frog Man

Once there was a little frog whose name was Freddie. He lived in a little pond on a little green lily pad with his mother and father.

Every day Freddy played with his friends and told them he wanted to grow up and become a little frog man. However, the other frogs laughed and teased and called Freddy a little frog baby.

One day machines came and made a pathway right through the pond while many were home relaxing on their respective lily pads. Some frogs including Freddie's father were killed. The homes were destroyed.

The next day Freddie kissed his mother and off he went looking for a new home. He traveled for a long time until he came to an old barn. He crawled through a hole in the side of the barn and found a small stack of hay. He laid down and took a nap. When he saw a big brown dog just growling and sniffing at him, Freddie was afraid, and he leaped away briskly. When he no longer heard the dog barking, he stopped and rested. Suddenly, the sky turned dark, and the storm came. Freddie stayed under a bush until the next morning. When he woke up, he heard the ducks splashing in a pond. He ran toward the sound and to his surprise he came upon the most beautiful pond full of lily pads.

Freddie immediately started on his journey back home. He found his mother and other frogs still gathered in the corner of the pond. He told them about the new community he discovered. The next day Freddie started on his second journey to lead his community to safety.

It was a long hard trip with many dangers, but the frogs made it to the new community safely. The frogs were so happy to find news homes. The frogs thanked and kissed Freddie. Then, the frogs jumped on chosen lily pads. Freddie had grown up overnight and he was longer known as the little baby frog but now he was a "big" frog man. Freddie lost his father. Then, he stepped up to the plate. Then, he became a responsible frog male leader.

Henry the Flying Horse

Henry was a beautiful black pony who always liked to run, jump, and play all day. He lived on a farm with two very nice people. Henry's owners did not have any children, so they often allowed the neighbor's kids to ride and play with Henry.

One Saturday morning, Jeff, the boy next door, who was Henry's best friend visited him. He took Henry down in the meadows and they played for a very long time. Jeff did not know Henry was a magic horse. Jeff started talking to Henry, but Henry kept right on running and playing and ignoring Jeff. Then, Jeff got Henry's attention and asked Henry a question.

Jeff asked Henry if he had one wish, what would that wish be?

Henry turned to him and replied, "I wish I could fly."

Jeff was frightened because Henry, a pony, talked to Jeff in a human voice. So, Jeff turned and ran away from Henry toward home.

That same night there was a terrible storm. The storm was so bad most of the farmhouses were damaged and Henry was gone. Jeff thought about Henry for a very long time. Finally, Jeff jumped up from his bed and ran to the neighbor's house where Henry lived but Henry still had not come home. Then Jeff ran to the meadows where he and Henry played. Henry was nowhere in sight. All Jeff could see was a giant lake which was formed by the storm. Jeff was afraid something happened to Henry. Then, he sat on the ground and cried.

Suddenly, Jeff stopped crying because he heard a strange sound. He turned and to his amazement he saw this beautiful black horse with the prettiest set of wings he had ever seen. The horse walked closer to him, and he realized it was Henry! He told Jeff that wishes sometimes come true if you believe in yourself. After Henry had spoken, he galloped faster and faster and he leaped into the air; as he flew away, Henry turned and waved to Jeff and yelled, "See you, my friend." Then, Henry flew off into the clouds.

The Crying Dog

There was once a little boy named David who loved animals, all kinds of animals, especially dogs. His parents did not allow him to have a pet dog because he was not old enough to take care of a pet on his own; so, David dreamed of owning his own dog.

One day David and his parents were driving through the country when he saw a dog in the road. It seemed like the dog appeared out of nowhere. The dog was lying there appearing to be crying and very sad. David immediately fell in love with the dog and pleaded with his dad, "Please let me take that dog home!" David's parents were so moved by his concern for the dog until they allowed him to the take the dog home.

In the following weeks, David and his family grew closer and closer to the dog. David tried everything to make the dog happy, but the dog cried a lot.

David named the dog Charlie in hopes of making the dog feel better. One day David took Charlie to a Little League game to introduce him to his friends and Charlie seemed excited. When David started to walk to the game, he did not see Charlie. He searched and searched but there was no sign of Charlie. David was tired so he started to walk down the road. David walked for hours desperately trying to find Charlie, but David soon realized he was lost, and he started crying.

Finally, David stopped crying because he heard

something crying louder. He turned and it was Charlie. He was tied up in a strange rope with a bright orange glow. David ran and untied Charlie and they both ran home as fast as they could. As the dog ran something strange happened. Charlie was changing from the sad little dog into a 10-year-old boy just like David. In amazement they both stopped cold and stood still. By the time the change was complete, as David looked at Charlie, he began to tell him how a witch cast a spell on him and turned him into a dog because he refused to give her money and the only way the spell could be broken was for someone to love Charlie unconditionally. So, since David loved Charlie as a dog, surely, he would love him as his friend.

They both walked home. No more tears and no more running away. David had a friend and Charlie had a home.

Tiny Tails

My name is James Robert. Early one morning, I woke up to a very strange sound. I got up and looked out my window, but I did not see anything. I went to the door and opened it. There to my surprise was the smallest dog I had ever seen. This was no puppy but a miniature dog. He had three brown legs and one white leg. I opened the door he ran inside. I noticed he had the smallest tail that stood up and slightly curved at the top. I ran behind him and picked him up. He could fit in the palm of my hand. He had the saddest brown eyes and I fell in love with him and immediately called him Tails.

I took Tails everywhere I went. I even took him to church on Sunday. Everyone who saw Tails fell in love with him. All the kids wanted to play with him.

One day I took Tails to the market. I turned for a minute to get his favorite dog food. When I turned around Tails was gone from the cart. I looked everywhere I looked for him but could not find him. After hours of searching, I gave up and went home.

I asked around but no one had seen him. The next day a little girl handed me a flier announcing a small carnival coming through our town at the end of the week. My friends and I decided to go. The day finally came so we went to the carnival. We had walked around for hours, and I was tired, so I looked for a place to sit. Finally, I found an empty bench. Suddenly, I heard a strange sound. I turned and looked across from me and saw something very small and helpless. I ran as fast as I could. There was my precious little dog caged and labeled "The World's Smallest Dog." He looked at me and I could tell he remembered me by his little barks. I pulled and tugged on the cage, but the manager pushed me away and called me a crazy kid. I was afraid, but I was not leaving without Tails. I searched for something that could help me set Tails free. I looked around and saw an open kitchen where I found a small knife. I opened the cage door and pulled Tails out. I stuck him in my coat pocket, and I ran all the way home! Tails had been missing for several months, but he was home now, and I will never let him go again!

Jacobie's Adventure

Once there was a little boy named Jacobie. He lived at home with his mother and father. Jacobie asked his father to buy him a go cart. He already had two bikes and many other toys that he did not play with. Dad finally agreed if Jacobie did well in school, he would buy him a go cart.

The summer came. Jacobie's grades were good, and his dad kept his word and bought the go cart. Jacobie only drove his go cart a few times and just like his other toys, he stored it in the backyard.

Mom was tired of Jacobie's neglect of his toys so she told him that if she neglected her car the way he did his toys it would fly away. The next day Jacobie went out to his mother's car and started to look at it very hard. He looked at the wheels and the trunk and even looked at the windshield. He looked at it very hard. He looked at the front of the car and noticed how the lights looked like two eyes. He moved from side to side and the car appeared to be looking at him. He thought he saw a tail at the back. After deciding he was just imaging things he turned to walk away. After taking a few steps he heard a growl. As he turned suddenly the car turned into a huge black cat with big yellow eyes. Jacobie was too afraid to speak so the cat said, "come with me." With a single paw he placed Jacobie on his neck and off they went into the air and through clouds.

As Jacobie sat on the huge cat's neck, he began to feel safe. They entered a strange city where there were no lights, no grass, no singing, just lots of sad toys. The cat blinked his huge eyes and told Jacobie that every time a child asks for toys and doesn't take care of them, their spirit comes to this place to live. Jacobie asked the cat to tell the name of the place where they were. The cat said the place did not have a name.

Jacobie promised the cat if it took him back home, he would take care of his toys that his parents worked so hard to give him and that he would thank them for his toys. At that moment the cat smiled and told him to hang on. In a few minutes Jacobie was home again. He climbed off the cat and thanked him for the adventure. The cat then rested. His feet became tires again, his eyes lights, and his tail disappeared altogether. It was no longer a huge black cat but mom's car again. Jacobie smiled and went inside to tell mom and dad all about his adventure.

Memories

Baby dolls and long jump-ropes,
Tennis shoes and toy rowboats.
True Romances stacked above the bed,
The telephone reminds me of the things I have said.
Sitting in the big oak tree,
Thinking of people, I wish I could be.
Holding hands with the neighbor's son,
Wishing tomorrow would never come.
Riding around as dad's little girl,
Lots of dreams to conquer the world.
Helping mom with the evening meal,
Saying my prayers by the bed as I kneel.
Married now with two little girls,
I still have dreams of conquering the world.
Memories are meant to keep close to the heart,
When old memories pass, new memories start.

3

Religious Poems

My Soul Mate

He is like a shadow,
within my shadow,
hidden,
but then,
showing himself for a minute,
then returning to my soul,
to remain hidden,
once again.

Death is a Castle

To start this life from birth,
to live throughout until our death,
has always been a mystery to me,
when your body is gone what is left?

Will our souls be here in the earth,
forever until judgement day,
or will our souls travel on,
to that castle bright and gay?

A castle of diamonds, silver and gold,
with beautiful flowers and trees so green,
with all the sights the mind could imagine,
more things than you have ever seen.

With stairs so tall they travel,
to all four corners of the earth,
with rooms so wide,
they hold all the world and births.

Death still frightens me sometimes,
I try to live the best I can,
for I know there is a castle waiting,
for me on Heaven's sand.

The Tears of God

Tap, tap, it starts to pour,
zoom, zoom, the wind will roar.

The trees are bent,
almost to the ground.
The birds fly away,
at the thundering sounds.

The earth is filled with puddles and streams.
The streets are wet,
no hope it seems.

Thunder and lightning,
and then comes rain,
to remind us once more,
that God is angry again.

Why must we anger Him so much,
that He shows His tears,
in the form of the wind,
and rain which we fear?

I know it sounds strange and maybe a little odd,
but the storms we fear,
are the tears of God.

The Eyes of God

Far, far away they hang right there,
one by day, and one by night,
hanging there without a thread,
standing there in perfect sight.

What an amazing sight it is,
to watch the setting of the sun.
What a wonderful feeling it is,
to watch the starlit morning.

Look at the sun as a new day begins.
Look at the moon as that same day ends.
They remind me so much of two huge eyes,
just hanging there in the middle of the skies.

Isn't it grand to realize,
that the moon and the sun,
are God's watchful eyes.

The Twelve Apostles

Peter preached the Gospel of Christ,
saying that baptism would pay the price.

Andrew asked, "how can we feed so many,
when at first, we didn't have any?"

James the son of Zebedee,
was present in the Garden of Gethsemane.
John caught a vision on the Lord's Day,
which showed us how we must study and pray.

Phillip after teaching gave Eunuch no choice,
but baptized him and sent him on his way full of joy.
Bartholomew was present in the upper room,
when the Holy Ghost fell up on them
with a great loud boom!
Thomas doubting that Jesus was alive,
stuck his hand through the hole in His side.
Matthew the tax collector of the city,
was asked to follow and showed no pity.
James the first apostle to see the risen Jesus,
is recorded as one who will help lead us.

Thaddaeus was one of the twelve in command,
preached the kingdom of heaven to all men.
Judas betrayed and caused Christ to die,
repented and hanged himself for that lie.
Paul fought hard with all his might,
but when life was ending said, "I have fought a good fight."

God Will See Me

I close my door with lock and key,
I make no sound because God will see me.

I close my Bible so I can be free,
I dare not open it because God will see me.

I walk around at night with head hanging down,
I watch my feet, so I won't make a sound.

I cover my ears and I cover my eyes,
I know somewhere beyond the skies.

There is a God who sees all things,
And with Him justice He brings.
I know none of these things will help me be free,
because God knows that I know He sees me.

4

Mystical Mini Short Stories

The Blue Water Lily

Drucenta was a young lady who lived at the edge of town. She had a beautiful flower garden every year.

One year, Drucenta decided to plant vegetables and flowers in the same garden. Big mistake. The only thing she found in her garden were rocks and large pieces of dirt. She was disappointed. Suddenly, she noticed something at the edge of the garden that looked strange. She walked to the plant and discovered a rare blue water lily full of blue pedals. It was beautiful. As she walked closer, there appeared to be two small eyes looking at her behind the pedal leaf. She concluded that what appeared to be eyes was not real.

Drucenta left the garden and went home. She went to bed but was awakened by a barking dog. She looked out her window and there was a strange blue haze coming from the garden. She went outside and walked over to the garden. She saw the blue image of a woman standing with her arms spread over the garden blessing the soil. Afterward, the blue image of the woman blew in the wind and vanished. Everything was dark and quiet. Therefore, Drucenta went back into her house and went to bed.

The next morning Drucenta woke up and went outside. She couldn't believe her eyes! There was her garden, all covered with roses, carnations, tulips, squash, tomatoes, pepper, and so on. The flowers and vegetables were sectioned off in rows in the garden. It was beautiful and she was so proud. Drucenta did not know what had happened; but she knew it had something to do with the blue image she saw in her garden.

She never saw the blue hazy image again but every year she was blessed with a beautiful garden of flowers and vegetables. Eventually, Drucenta realized the eyes she saw that night behind the blue water lily belonged to the woman who blessed the garden soil.

.

The Farmer's Market

Joe Marie was a very kind lady who lived in a small town in Aldoza, Kingston. After years of bad weather, storms, draught, and frequent floodings the town was left with few businesses. Most of the residents moved to other towns to survive. In fact. there was only a gas station, two small grocery stores, one clothing store, and the main business was the farmer's market.

Jo Marie was determined to support the farmer's market and to encourage her neighbors. Every day she went to the Farmer's Market, one of the last functioning businesses left to buy fruits and vegetables and share them with neighbors.

One day she went to the market and bought her usual supplies and walked through town sharing her fruits and vegetables. This time she gave out too much without realizing she was only left with what she thought was a melon. Since that was all she had left she took it home. She sat the basket on the table. Then, she opened the basket and noticed the melon was changing colors from green to orange and then yellow. The melon gleamed like a streak of lighting and then it started spinning, spinning, spinning, and growing. By this time, Joe Marie realized the melon was going to burst. So, she ran and locked herself in her closet. Then she heard a very loud noise and then silence.

Joe Marie was afraid to open the closet door. She fell asleep and slept in the closet all night. The next morning, she woke up, walked out of the closet and she could not believe her eyes or recognize her house because it was covered with gold pieces. There was more gold scattered around her house than she could have ever imagined seeing in her lifetime.

She went back to town, told the people in the community about her newfound fortune and she agreed to share her fortune with the town of Aldoza to help with the recovery process. She went back home picked up the gold pieces and placed them in a large suitcase.

The gold was sold. Funds were used to rebuild the town. The residents returned and obtained jobs building new schools, stores, homes, and other structures and working in the new businesses.

Joe Marie was praised by the whole town. The construction crew built a large house in the middle of town in Joe Marie's honor. The grounds included a courtyard and a park with picnic tables. Everyone was happy again, especially Joe Marie.

Joe Marie volunteered most of her days working at the Farmer's Market because she was thankful that the magic melon and the gold saved the town. No one owed any loans for their homes and buildings and Joe Marie was debt free.

Bella and the Magic Painting

Bella was a young artist who constantly worked at different art galleries showing off her artwork with average success; she was always discouraged by nay sayers who told her she would never be great in her craft. Instead of allowing Bella to paint and grow as an artist, the gallery owners gave Bella a support staff position and duties such as running errands and making coffee.

One day Bella went to work and expressed her passion to be an artist and asked the owner to allow her to draw a few paintings. The owner laughed at Bella and assured her she was not ready to become a painter. Bella was deeply hurt by his rejection. She cried and ran out of the gallery and never returned. She was determined to prove to herself and the world that painting was her destiny. She decided to paint the ultimate portrait to show the nay sayers that they were wrong.

She went home and started her journey to create the ultimate painting and after many failures she gave up and decided not to try anymore.

One morning Bella woke up with a strange desire to resume her painting. She did not know what to paint so she just started painting. It was like her hands were being guided by a force outside of herself.

She painted that whole morning. After that strange feeling left her she realized she had painted a beautiful forest with unusual trees, flowers, grass, birds, and a small stream running beside the trees.

She thought it was very pretty because the colors were so beautiful until they looked real. In fact, too real, so she touched the picture, and she could feel the water running; she could hear the birds singing, and she could smell the flowers. Bella realized the painting was alive!

Bella had to sit for a moment and think about what was happening. What does this mean? She concluded that this was an incentive from God to encourage her to keep painting.

Bella started painting again and became very successful. Anytime she felt like her work was slowing down she touched the painting, and she continued drawing and her ideas flowed.

As for her live painting, she never told anyone about it. She just kept it in her room for comfort and encouragement. The flowers smelled sweet, and the bird's songs were so calming until she kept that piece of her blessing all to herself.

The Crystal Vase

I see the Crystal Vase sitting in the middle of the room. It contains flowers. They look like Roses. Six white, six yellow and six red. Some represent sadness in my life. Some represent the high points of my life, growing up, marriage and having my babies. I can't tell if the vase is half empty or half full. It just sits there in the middle of the room - still, shining, and quiet. I wonder what the crystal vase is thinking. I wonder if it plans to add more roses. I don't understand how something so simple as a crystal vase with totally different colors of flowers can be both beautiful and sad at the same time.

I see you Crystal Vase, even though my eyes are closed, I still see you. And you see me. God sent you to remind me of the things that are beautiful but sad to enjoy.

Thank you, God, for sending me the Crystal Vase, filled with memories, sitting in the middle of the room which I can see even with my eyes closed remembering precious moments.

The Angel Child

Cassondra was a proud young lady who lived through many difficult moments in her life. She had no parents or living relatives. Her husband, Wesley, died from his injuries during a deer hunting accident and she never had kids, but she wanted them desperately.

She was always going to the market and picking up different things on the way like berries, peaches, pears, and even rocks. One day she stumbled across an old house on her way home which she had never seen before. She walked to the door; it was cracked opened; so, she walked inside. Home décor and clothes were spread on the floor. A couch was upside down against the wall.

The house was extremely messy, and it smelled like burnt ashes from the fireplace even though none of the structure was burned. Cassondra continued to walk through the house and stopped when she reached the kitchen. The kitchen was a wreck too. Broken dishes were scattered on the kitchen floor. Leftover food was on the stove. The kitchen curtains were torn. Dirty water was in the kitchen sink.

Cassondra looked under the kitchen table and she could not believe her eyes. There was a large bubble under the table containing a female infant balled up in a fetal position. Although Cassondra was frightened; she could not leave that bubble. She picked it up, ran out of the house, and took the bubble home.

She put the bubble in her extra bedroom and covered it up with a blanket. She was confused and needed to think so she went to bed and fell asleep. She slept for what seemed like a long time but finally she woke up. She remembered the bubble and ran to the room! The bubble contained a small baby girl. The bubble busted. Cassondra picked her up and there was a tiny set of wings on her back. Cassondra immediately felt love for the baby.

Cassondra natured and cared for the child as she began to grow and grow. She started to walk and talk just like any other child, but she had wings. Cassondra knew that this was no ordinary child and that she could never truly be hers. She understood that she would have to give her up some day. She named the child, "Angel Child." Cassondra kept Angel Child close to her. Cassondra explained to her neighbors Angel Child was left on her doorstep.

As Angel Child grew and attended school, she was always the smartest child there throughout her school years. Soon she taught her mother how to raise her vegetables and crops better and how to use the money wisely and how to shop when she went to the market for goods. Since Angel Child was so good with numbers, Cassondra and Angel Child opened a bookkeeping business. The business became lucrative; they became wealthy. They moved into a new house and were able to save a lot of money.

Cassondra noticed the physical changes of Angel Child. Her hands became larger, and her wings spread wider. The neighbors noticed the hands, but they never saw the wings which were hidden beneath Angel Child's loose-fitting outfits. Cassondra knew it would soon be time to say goodbye to Angel Child. Her time was running out.

One morning Cassondra was awakened by a strange sound. She set up in the bed and looked out the window. The sun was so bright until she could hardly see. Finally, she saw Angel Child starring up at the sky. There was a second sun shining and she had her hands stretched forward. Suddenly, the second sun opened, her wings spread, and she rose from the ground. Angel Child realized Cassondra was watching; then, she turned and said, "I love you," and she waved goodbye.

That was the last time Cassondra saw Angel Child. However, Cassondra was not sad because she knew Angel Child was not here to stay and Angel Child fulfilled Cassandra's dream of motherhood. Their bond brought Cassondra so much joy and love until she never felt alone again.

Shelby/Shana

There was once a little girl called Shelby. She lived in a smalltown called Spring Peaks. During the spring season, the hills looked like upside-down ice cream cones. Shelby was happy living with her mom and dad and baby sister Skyy. Shelby was so excited about finally starting school. Little did she know that life for her would change forever. From the very beginning of school, she was bullied by the children because they felt she was oddly different.

As she grew up her features became stronger and stronger. She had extremely red hair, very thick and dry skin and eyes that seemed far too big for her face; her feet were oversized and hands that did not fit her body.

Most of the children and some of the staff were uncomfortable around her; no one wanted to be her friend! All through her school years, certain children did awful things to her such as pulling the chairs from under her to locking her in the dressing room during the class period. Shelby complained to her parents, but nothing ever got solved. Even the teachers would not help her because she was so different. Finally, she entered her senior year, and little did she know this would be her worst year yet.

The children were returning to school from the summer break, and the bullying resumed immediately; the same group of children dumped their lunches in her lap in the cafeteria and formed a circle around her and would not let her leave.

A new teacher who did not know the history of the school walked up and made that group of children leave and she helped Shelby to the bathroom to clean up. Shelby started crying and screaming as she explained what her life had been like. The teacher felt awful and promised Shelby she would try to help her through this final year. Things got a little better with Ms. Elliott looking after her; as a matter of fact she became Shelby's first friend.

A few weeks passed and Shelby started feeling better about herself, until she was approached by several girls at the end of class. This time they did not want to torment her but instead they wanted to invite her to a pool party at the local park. Shelby was excited!

Shelby showed up at the party alone. The group of girls whose names were Dana, Melissa, and Breanna were there and immediately came over to greet her. Shelby was so excited about finally being accepted by some of her peers. By then, her hands and feet were physically larger. Her eyes were very deep, and her freckles would not stop. But what she hated most of all about her appearance was her extremely thick skin; she could fall and never bleed or never get a bruise; during the summer she stayed sweaty because she could never cool off.

The party finally speeded up and everybody jumped into the pool including Shelby. Suddenly, the group of girls jumped on Shelby and held her down until she stopped breathing. They all let go and jumped out of the pool and left Shelby at the bottom of the pool and they scattered and ran away laughing! It was their intent all along to kill Shelby.

Ms. Elliot was in the kitchen helping with the food when she heard the screaming and laughter. She came out running; all the children ran away, and Shelby was at the bottom of the pool appearing to be dead.

Ms. Elliot jumped in the pool and dragged Shelby out! She was not dead but unconscious. Ms. Elliot performed CPR and Shelby responded. She assisted Shelby to walk into the kitchen. Shelby became hysterical, screaming and crying; she hated the girls for being evil toward her. She screamed and she hated herself. Suddenly, she grabbed a knife off the table and started cutting herself. She cut and cut and cut! But she did not bleed.

Instead, she grabbed a piece of her skin and started pulling it off. She peeled and peeled and peeled until she realized she had peeled her skin off. After that she looked at her face and hair and she peeled it off too. She realized she had turned into two people; one of her persons was inside the other.

She ran to the bathroom and looked at herself. She was beautiful. Just plain beautiful!

Ms. Elliot watched with anticipation but did not interfere and was not shocked.

Shelby finally turned to Ms. Elliott, and she realized Ms. Elliott knew all about her.

They begin to talk, and Ms. Elliot told her she was also born the same way. She told her the story of how her mother and two sisters had moved her from the Fenestra Islands and they each had a child within a child, and she was in fact her cousin.

Shelby was still angry about all those times she was bullied. But most of all, she was angry at how those girls who tried to kill her, ran away laughing, and got away with it. Shelby decided something must be done to the girls who tortured her. Shelby was the only person willing to do anything to the girls.

Ms. Elliott returned to school the next morning as if nothing happened. When asked what happened to Shelby, she just simply said she did not know. The same day a new girl Shana came to school. She became popular especially with the group that left her for dead at the bottom of the pool.

One day Shana came to school as usual after class they all spent time together. Shana suggested they spend the weekend in her parent's summer cottage and just chill. All four agreed.

Dana, Melissa, and Breanna met up that weekend and went to a log cabin. They watched movies, listened to music, danced, ate pizza and had the time of their lives. That night after everyone went to bed. Shana went to each room and tied them to their beds.

The next morning after each girl woke up, she

realized she was not able to move. Dana, Melissa, and Breanna realized they had been tricked and started screaming. Shana revealed herself to them and reminded them what they had done to her. For three days she tortured them. She did not give them any food, and very little water. The girls were given few bathroom breaks; they were not allowed to change clothes. Ms. Elliot was the only person who knew where the girls were. But Ms. Elliot was not aware that Shana was torturing the girls. The girls cried and pleaded day and night but Shelby would not bulge.

On the fourth morning the girls woke up and found they were free. Shelby burned their shoes, so they walked through the woods barefooted. They reached the highway, got a ride and made it to their homes safely. Shelby was never heard from again.

One day Ms. Elliott received a card from the Fenestra Island. Yes, it was Shelby, and she was still beautiful, and she had reunited with her family and was very happy.

Note: Written by Rose Burkett 03.03.21

The X-Tra Water Bottle

There was a boy named John Moses who lived in a small town called Albany Springs with his mother and sister. Everyday John Moses had to care for his sister while his mother worked at the local bakery. Although she worked long hours, there never seemed to be enough money, and something was always needed especially water.

One day John Moses was picking up his sister from school when he saw an elderly lady walking with her arms full of groceries. She told him if he would help her with her groceries, she would give him a bottle of water. He agreed and he took her groceries home.

John Moses and the lady became very good friends. He even nicknamed her "The Water Lady" and carried her groceries for her every week afterward. Time went on, John Moses grew up and went off to college. His mother and sister moved away, and he never saw the "Water Lady" again.

One day John Moses got a letter in the mail, and he could not believe who it was from. Yes, "The Water Lady." She was very sick and in the hospital. The letter said she desperately wanted to see him.

He immediately went to see her. She was so happy when he walked into her room. They talked about their visits and how he never left without that X-tra bottle of water. She became very quiet for a while. Then, she reached under her pillow and pulled out some papers. She explained that she was a widow and she never had children. She was very wealthy, and he was her only family now. She informed him she was leaving her earthly treasures to him in her Last Will and Testament!

She reached under her pillow again, pulled out an X-tra bottle of water which become the last bottle of water she gave her dear friend John Moses!

She smiled, closed her eyes, and went to Heaven.

John Moses was happy because he learned the meaning of true friendship. One who can never forget you even when they have passed away. He smiled, kissed her cheek, and said "Good-bye."

He never forgot their times together and the love she showed him and would never forget "The Water Lady" and that X-tra bottle of water.

Grandmother's Promise

Grandmother and I were very close. So, on the day of my wedding, she baked me this huge seven-layer cake with pink frosting. This cake was very pretty and it was large enough for the whole family and guest to eat.

In a rush to leave for my honeymoon I missed getting a piece of the cake. I was away for four days. By the time I came back home all the cake was gone.

I always love Grandmother's cakes. So, I told her I did not get any cake. Grandmother promised me that she would bake another cake just for me.

Shortly after that grandmother became very ill and remained ill for some time.

One evening the telephone rang, grandmother had been taken to the hospital.

She remained unconscious until the angels came for her the next day. My heart ached. Her death was so hard to accept until I could not eat or sleep. After days of restlessness, I finally settled down and went to sleep.

My grandmother came to me in a dream carrying this huge pink and white cake. She cut a slice and handed it to me. It was so good! It was delicious just like all her cakes. I wanted another slice, so I asked for another slice. She turned to me and said, "Baby you will never taste this cake again," and she left.

When I woke up, I realized grandmother had found a way to keep her promise to me. Even in death she still loved me.

I will never forget that dream because it still fills my heart with love and joy.

The Blue Diamond Necklace (Train Wreck)

It all happened one evening during the summertime. Haley was on her way to spend the summer with her aunt in Myles Cove. As she boarded the train, she noticed two very well-dressed ladies who greeted her very politely and wished her a good day.

She boarded the train in a hurry to get to her seat and call her aunt. Surprisingly, she noticed the two ladies were seated directly behind her and she was very pleased.

The train started to move, and everyone just chattered among themselves. The two ladies talked among themselves and from time to time shared their conversation with Haley. That is when Haley admired a beautiful silver necklace, set in several blue diamonds, hanging on one of the lady's neck.

After admiring the necklace, Haley fell asleep but was awaken by awful noises. She realized the train had wrecked and everything was in a disarray. People were screaming. She wondered if the two ladies were safe but did not see them.

Everything happened so fast! Passengers were being removed from the train; lights were flashing, water was flowing, and first responders were walking back and forth.

During all the commotion Haley managed to see two of the passengers taken off the train. Yes, to her sorrow the two ladies she befriended were taken off the train deceased in stretchers. In a flash Haley remembered the blue diamond necklace. It was missing! She could not see it anywhere.

After that Haley was quickly whisked off by the paramedics and fell unconscious. The next morning, she woke up in the hospital with nonthreatening injuries. She felt so sad for the two ladies. She had not had the opportunity to learn their names.

After a couple of days, she was discharged from the hospital and decided to inquire about the ladies. She learned they were two sisters traveling abroad, and they were rich Heiresses. Just before she left the hospital the employees from the train station delivered the ladies' luggage to Haley. Before the train wrecked, the ladies had stuffed the necklace Haley admired in her suitcase.

Haley's aunt picked her up and carried her home. After a few hours of rest Haley decided to unpack her luggage. To her surprise there it was that beautiful blue diamond necklace stuffed in the pocket of her suitcase! The lady must have sensed she would not survive the train wreck and placed the necklace there.

Haley shouted to her aunt to come to her room. She explained the whole story to her aunt because she did not know what to do. Haley called the authorities and to find out if she could keep the expensive jewelry. Haley turned the necklace over to the authorities. The authorities investigated the story. Haley was given the necklace which was worth a great deal of money. Haley had the necklace appraised. Then, she sold it to a diamond collector. The funds from the sale were enough to buy a beautiful home and an automobile for Haley and her aunt. Haley was even able to pay tuition to obtain a college degree. Haley became a successful attorney and she and her aunt lived very comfortably. But she never forgot that tragic day that brought two nameless people in her life for a few minutes. The blue diamond necklace gift charged her life forever.

Haley hung a plaque in her office on the wall which reminded her of her blessing from the lady on the train. An image of the plague is below:

"No one knows how their journey will end. But that end is in the hands of God."

The Bumble Bee That Had No Stripes

Becky was a beautiful bumble bee. She was kind and sweet and had a lot of friends. But Becky sometimes felt a little shy because they all had stripes and Becky had none. Even when Becky went to Honeycomb High School, she found herself alone because her friends were embarrassed to be with her.

Now it was the middle of the year and time for the annual Bee-Hop dance. All the bees came to this dance. Becky, Bonnie and Betty were the best of friends and they met at the table for lunch every day. They talked about the dance, and their dates. Becky had not been asked but she was sure that Brian would ask her. But as the day went on, he never came near her. Becky went home heart broken.

A week passed and finally on the day of the dance, Becky had no date, so she told the class she was not attending the dance.

They all felt so sorry for Becky. Becky went home and locked herself in her room and cried for a long time. Suddenly, the wind started to blow very hard until it seemed to be knocking at the window. Becky began to feel afraid, so she ran over to the window to lock it. She reached for the lock but stopped cold. There stood this giant bee. She had gold stripes in her wings, a wand in her hand, and yellow halo over her head. She looked at Becky for a long time. Becky no longer felt afraid. Finally, she told Becky to close her eyes and turn three full circles on the floor. The bee told Becky to open her eyes and look down. To Becky's surprise, she had the prettiest set of black stripes that any bee could have. She was so excited that she turned and ran to show her strips to her mother.

In her excitement, she forgot to thank her Fairy god bee, but when she turned the bee smiled and vanished. Becky ran down the stairs to her mother.

Becky was proud of herself. She finally got her stripes. But she felt sad again. She went down to watch television. Then there was a knock at the door. Mother bee opened the door. Becky turned and there was the whole bunch from Honeycomb High School with Bonnie and Betty leading the way.

They all told Becky how sorry they were for making her feel left out and they all agreed to move the dance to her house.

Becky was very happy; she turned on the music, set up the table and everyone started dancing. The best part of the evening was Becky and Brian dancing to her favorite song.

ABOUT THE AUTHOR

Rose Humphrey Burkett, a native of Flora, Madison County, Mississippi, is a published poet. *Teacup Memories* is her first complete work. Burkett is an administrative assistant in the medical field. She holds a degree in Medical Administration from Hinds Community College. The author lives in Jackson, Hinds County, Mississippi with her husband A. Jerry Burkett.

Made in the USA
Columbia, SC
19 February 2023

12686206R00039